A Shadow in Yucatán

(A Tale Sung in Exile)

by

Philippa Rees

Cover design: Philippa Rees, Ana Grigoriu
Book Interior: Philippa Rees

Photographs: Cover image and pages
3,5,10,12,35,54,55,62,68,74,80,82,85,102,110
www.crestock.com
Pages 22,24,26,29,34,37,40,45,47,51,58,70,72,78,93,99
www.shutterstock.com

First Print Edition 2006

This Edition Published by:
CollaborArt Books

ISBN 978-0-9575002-3-5

Dedicated to the Nameless Girl.

El Progresso was further than the back of beyond. It was the flywhisk refuge of the poor waiting for winter work and the sharks that cruised past in hope of the equally unlikely; a dry landscape of fathomless cenotes and human sacrifice.

Here in pitiless sun this tale was spilt, by a troubadour of sorts, a girl who had fled her past, blindly and in pain. I have written it for her, and for others that remember the eclipse of joy. The setting has been changed; the characters are fictitious, but our betrayal was universal. We were betrayed by our hunger for hope.

This song is a lament.

'I was utterly awestruck by the writing skill and breadth of imaginative evocation.....poetic, elegiac...almost unbearably intense...sensuous imagery from both nature and modern urban living...musical, both rhythmic and assonant...sustained dramatic tension within a simple everyday story....the superficiality of the beauty salon is a very potent metaphor....'

Alison Jakes (Poetry Circle)

As with a highly literary novel, this ambitious story makes demands upon its readers. As with most modern poetry it deserves to be read and re-read.....

The story is a vehicle for some impressive poetry. It is highly emotional and transforms the ordinary protagonist into an archetypal figure of suffering motherhood.

'Speech must now grow from silence and the stones that cockle the black backs
Of women in pre-history, left alone with the consequence of men'

There is religious dimension too. Throughout there are subtle references to the Christian Nativity, and on another level it tells of Christ's birth and Mary's suffering in modern terms. It contrasts the cruelty of the girl's Catholic mother, with the compassion of her Jewish landlady.

There is implicit criticism of the hypocrisy of society as a whole....The poem has a social purpose.

Katherine Knight (Real Writers)

Philippa Rees is as an immediately distinctive and striking poet who writes with unfashionably – often brilliant – painterly verbal play and colour, oozing with a sensuous love of language. Rees's almost tangible style dazzles with imagistic chiaroscuro; stark contrasts of light and shade, subtext and texture:

This ripeness of verbiage and intrinsic musicality inevitably bring comparisons with Dylan Thomas (particularly the densely descriptive, rumble-tumble list- passages of Under Milk Wood):
But this is not to detract from Rees's individuality, which, throughout this book of poetic narrative interspersed with colourful dialogue, is palpable and often beguiling. She is prone to the lingering aphorism that is imaginatively her own—

Lethargy, that toothless crone, skims perpetual
indifference from the cream of richer care.

...the drifting necklace of leaves that swung
from the throat of shade

For my part, I read A Shadow in Yucatán mainly for its poetry, its play with language, image and sound, rather than strictly trying to follow the actual narrative. Approaching this book with a sort of Negative Capability, I experienced it in terms of descriptive impression, verbal effect. In this respect, A Shadow in Yucatán is disarmingly beautiful

(Alan Morrison, Editor The Recusant)

The back blurb calls 'A Shadow in Yucatán' a 'distilled novel' and it is –a home brew, raw and omnipotent! Rees makes extraordinary the sorrowful ordinary of an unwanted pregnancy and the resulting difficult decisions. She celebrates the sense of community, despairs of family and counts on the generosity of strangers. She explores problems and finds solutions – hard through they are to take – in unexpected places

Through it we enter a world as real as we are, but as foreign to us as a bad dream. This book is a must for any intelligent reader!

(Independent Reviews: SP Magazine)

The Beauty Parlour, Coconut Grove

All day the cycles swing around the window,
the tanned legs flattered by the double glass
then arrested...Ratchets buzz impatient...
The slow generator arbitrates...
The green light frees the traffic's undertow.

Reflected twice, the lightweight English Raleighs,
gears, toe-clips, nudge the dryers against the far
white wall.
Wink and seduce the gap-toothed rubber plant,
skewer Mrs. Sklayne at her pedicure, with spokes.

'Not too short at back...mind the kiss curl's at the side...
let me remove my spectacles...'

'Vogue or Harpers, take ya pick?
Will y'ave coffee, chocolate or iced milk?'

Stephanie works fast, (*she's real nice Steph...*)
not smart y'hear, but steady, plain but clean;
her fair-isle sweater under the gingham darned at
the elbow,

'But the ankles, it's a shame, a shade too thick.
She's been with us, let's see...goin on three years
and as I recall, never a day missed...
Quiet with the customers, never chatty...that sort
leave...
Ten fifty altogether...have a nice day...'

'Where the hell's that cheeseburger?
'I jus gotta have a cigarette'

....

'Are you early lunch or late?'

Stephanie shrugs, her wide mouth full of pins.
She fixes the bangs, sprays and dusts the neck...
powder tin is empty...

'Drugstore'll be crowded'

'I'll eat my apple in the park'

'Yeah? Well suit y'self. I'm blowin. Gotta rip.'

....

The tide is out, the grass worn summer-thin.
The cymbal-shakin Hare Krishna set have gone to swim.
The wind is blowin west, there ain't one jib,
the burgees up the masts a yelpin din...
The pelicans have gone.

'Christ I feel sick!'

Wally's in his hammock with his kids,
his squint son, bored with bark, with woodlice,
and the tethered tree.
His daughter sunk in her talcum sleep is stroked...

The monocle of light, now focussed, flames her
hair, it lifts, it falls, it curves, conceals...
Her open nectar-mouth, now shaded, breathes.

He peers between his knees into the dust
unable to distinguish screw from seed...
He sifts with fingers, looks beneath his thigh,
investigates the folds of sock, and sighs...

Balanced on one palm he rolls erect and goes to
pull a rush leaf by the hedge,
splits it with his neat sharp teeth,
curves length along an easy tongue...
Binds his bifocal frames with green,
and sits back down.

Now he takes up and tunes a steel banjo.
His hands, with nails kept short, are competent
and quick.
They guide the dolphin sounds through hoops of
tree; he bends, he turns, harks with ear inclined...
It reaches pitch. It thrums and calls...he seldom
plays, he keeps it tuned, in case.

He's come far, has Wally, in the years, come
March, since Annie rode away astride a pillion,
arms around her black...OK her darkie...(Nigger if
y'like)
Shacked up in Oregon...he isn't sure.
She does not often write.

The kids, the bike, banjo, all-purpose knife,
comprise his got-together, self-sufficient life.

'I ain't sold'

Stephanie's doubts confuse, her hopes weave
round and round.
She's walking straight, though slowly, on the shore
queasy as that oil slick on the sand

'Tar barrels, fish and quarrelling gulls sure don't help
me stomach varnish, acetone and cream...
His small girl needs a mama, that's for sure...
I'd bake us pizza, we could cut cookies..

'I'm gonna be sick!'

Wally stops.
He knows the scene.

Man, that's too much!
That girl beyond the sawgrass...she's alone...
an why she's bending down so low?

Her back convulses, shows its spine, and spews...
The gulls come circling...
peck, startled, skid the retch recoil,
relentless pump, the thud.

She's fallen on her knees...no she gets up...
she's goin to splash her face in curvin brine.

Discards her sandals, rinses and then spits...She
spits twice more.
Enjoys the tang of salt, the clear clean sting
of salt, of salt, of salt...
A welling unimpeded view of everything.

'Yer pregnant ain't ya?'

Wally's all concern.
For all his hard won sinew, he's a family man.
He loves his children, loves his loving too...

'Honest, I don know'

Fearing another bout with bile, she half turns
away.

Slowly redeemed, her shoulders sink; the sulky sea turns chill.
The strutting flicking feathers hunch. The shadows too blanch dim...
Evaporating light...the light holds everything

She thought she saw...
His eyes see emptying.

....

A candid light returns, a flood-lamp sun, angled to define both weight and line.
Her sweating hands smooth skirt, and fasten shoe...
He plants his feet still deeper in the mud

'Oughta find out soon'

He scratches an elbow.
She bends her head.
A dried reed rattles. A lifting sail subsides...

'It's no good hangin out. What is, is bound t'be...
I know a doc, works way up-town, a regular medic, not some knife happy loon
I don suppose you'd go to y' own.
If you drive up past Funland, past the ole dry dam...
Tell you what, come back. I'll write it down.'

Stephanie follows, servile, blind, searching for water through her seeping mind...

The sea, the sky, and buried somewhere under
salt...the effervescent tongue refreshing view...
But in the distance, at her feet, she sees
only a child asleep.

A banjo, a bag, split, full of diapers, nuts and
mixed dried fruit...
a diet for a life, the open road.
The weightless child asleep, and loneliness the
load.

She folds the paper, thanks him, leaves him to the
leaves, and goes.

....

Two saffron monks, pale-pated, cross the grass.
Their discourse falls in folds, their hands elaborate,
perennial truth perhaps...
(Perhaps the price of rice.)
The shafted pencil-light writes clearly on their
crowns; the ankles trace the shadows, but the bare
feet laugh...

Avid for a taste of their measured paced-out peace,
Stephanie picks an unripe lime.
Bites bravely through its grim green skin...
The eyes goddam-it water, the astringent palate
smarts...
She sucks at it regardless...squeezing and recoiling,
she kicks off her shoes...disdains the easy
somersault, accepts the broken glass...

'It's good, it's good, someways it's great! I'm dressed in polished poplin...Inside I feel all new...'

Then euphoria hits the sidewalk. She begins to smooth her hair.

The sleek glass door is guillotine to any thoughtless tread...
The receptionist surveys any likely unwashed head...
Stephanie is pole-axed, overpowered, drained
by air-conditioned talcum, re-circulated scent,
plushy velvet drapes, glossy blown-up prints.

Ye Gods is this the morgue? Must I undertake the corpse?
Lacquer for internment, ritual oils and masks...
Go daub your dead with war paint
let' em paddle their own hearse.

'Why there y'are honey...Mrs. Beale's in number three...
She says she's pushed for time...make it snappy, there's a dear...
Just a wash and shingle...no, today no facial hair...'

Thank God tomorrow's Friday. I'll just get through this week.

'Say please pass my lighter..and Joe?...out back...Joe! Joe!

Oh Joe, order lemon tea.

Saturday

Twenty-eighth street South, holds credit potential
and promise.
Once a grove of palms, rattling perpetually...
Now a lattice, plotted on points, two trees to each
house, each pruned to the axis of the unfettered
cable...
Only the occasional fruit, silently ripening...seed
accurate...
The perpendicular plumb-line bomb

(A small cycle was found crumpled in the cover it
bucked into un-steered; a hedge in bloom with
passion flowers...)

Often enough to latch-key mind, whether to call
the tree man?
Or wait for the hurricane?

This is the old quarter of the Grove, built
when folks were bright with hope and standards
before the boom and greenback brass...
They were clean shaven then, and not too clever,
they built small with chain link fences,
they laid paths and still sink flowers.

(Five years, on average, before a sleek Estate is
parked fenceless further south, protected by the
German Shepherd and strolling Securicor.)

*'It's nearer to the beach y'know, and Arthur? Why, he
doesn't mind the drivin'*

Twenty-eighth on Saturday sleeps late, or walks
the dog...
No Afghan or elegant Saluki, but a home-grown
sensible get-down Rover part pet and part
policeman.
Sniffing its beat from Hibiscus to Azalea,
sneezing, pausing, lifting and retracing...
Tangling skeins of trotted scent along the clipped
grass sidewalk, four blocks to the Causeway,
and once over, to the Bay.

Man, now see him move!

At seven the street is a long lick of paint.
The Banyan boon of shade at the corner belongs to the Architect.
(His curved walls are cedar, all other walls are white.)
No tooth shadows gnaw the surfaces as they do at noon:
The tattered spikes that serve the night are raised portcullis high, but the garrison is in its vest, and the mailman's been and gone.

Now the sun is cracked for breakfast in the middle of the street; spatters the sidewalk, and the back of the newsboy's knees...
Only sleep soiled quarters grey and dim, door hatches plastic sealed...
The air-propeller din sucked greedily through straw of mesh and spat across the sheet.

'Hey Honey? D'ya hear me? Would you say that fella's queer?
Y' know that one that wears those shorts and those shades against the glare?'

....

Stephanie stirs to the flapping of sheets, and the creaking revolution of a line...
Slatted sun flickers...
The windowsill flares, and is doused by the closing eye.
The open palm reflexes, the pillow wrist reclines, her body curves towards its plinth and melts again in sleep.
The clock-still, washer-numb, rag-bound Sabbath sulks.

Mrs. Martins in mules beneath the mangoes treads a protest in sand and suds across to the line and back.
Shuffles to stay shod, slaps and damns the mosquitoes.

Body bowls fall un-harnessed, roll beneath the
housecoat...
(blessed midges take advantage in the shade)

She feels for a pocket of pegs, spins, secures, spins
and reaches, and scratching a buttock tracks back.
Mrs. Martins is shaking her Sabbath fist. Shalom.

'So Abel how does it look? It looks good huh?
Your auntie, Abel, on the Sabbath in rollers, at the
mangle maybe?
To honour that wheedling whippet, long-legged lay-
about, your uncle Will
(not will enough to stay alive even.) Not that I am
noticing the difference...
him half buried in the fishing canoe, paddling lazy
through the saw-grass with his pipe...
Did she ever tell you (your mama with her shoes and
hats) that your uncle was an alligator?
But still Abel, how does it look? I should also be
enjoying the hats, and today dressing for Schul'

Miriam, widow of goy Wilbur, continues to
soliloquize without malice.
Wilbur, cause of curses has been dead too long.

Abel, adulated heir, prepares for manhood.
The uncertain Sabbath must be monitored;
he consults his gold Rolex, picks his nose and turns
the pages of a comic he is not reading...

'So why must he read when he inherits an apartment north of Fontainebleu?'

'Ah, the tenant is awake. I will ask when the flushing has a decent interval. If I could bring myself to eat bacon, we could be having breakfast. A daughter I wish I had. To adopt I couldn't afford; to make believe costs a person nothing.'

The Specialist

Synchronised signals on Lauderdale thread the
lace of the idling engine...
A line up of short-order shacks elbows for a view
of the parade.

Champ beats Burger-king, knocked down to Pete's
Pizzas, and two to you from Charlie's Cornets...
(bigger you can't buy)

Stand aside. Yonder Palm Beach...
(cut rates for condominium convenience)

'For a place near the water, what's ninety thousand
bucks?
We need to moor the catamaran, honey'

Well before.
Before the Boulevards, and Porcelain Parlour,
Cassata Cafe and Originals by Appointment, the
Florida fanfare is scored for braggart brass,
despairing cheerfulness...

Flaggin y'down with a swollen tongue...
Only one, jus one more soda from de poor,
the undimmed Pepsodent poor

One hundred eighty sixth street, north?
Right. Four blocks later, left.
Another street, undistinguished, communal grass,
paved ways, porticos; hedge-less by decree...

'Colonial rambling' developers would call it
(spreading their signet rings to cast the shadows of
illimitable oaks and graciousness)
'All that in two pillars and a porch, anodized,
weatherized, and warranted for two years against rust.'

....

Dr. Paul Robsart lurks behind the tiger blind in
button-down battledress and horn-rims

'He'll have ya believin Memphis is in Massachusetts'

Chimes strike salad welcome, daily-dozen, apple-
a-day ratio of health.
Visitors are here through carelessness,
the air-conditioning primed for punishment

'Take a seat honey. We'll need to take y'details'

The mother reluctant crosses adolescent knees.
The off-white chairs are carefully squared,
the carpet piled like straw.
The face behind the glass is gashed, and continues
to dry its nails...

....

'The Name of the Father?'

The apostrophe in the perplexed gut?

The sleeping spawn alive and palpitating asks for no father...

'Profession of the Father?'

What did the man profess?
That smooth sweet talker, un-confessing party fella, the walk-away soft-spoken con, gentle enough in loving, nice enough, no more...

'I think he Represents...'

'Name of the Mother?'

Ah me? I have a name?
I, the spreading shade of passing pleasure, I am never asked...
A dusted delicacy of quick consumption. I carry the name of Nature; wax like a ruddy redwood to let fall one perfect seed.
Must I needs also a name?

'Stephanie de Steffano'

'That's real purty. I like that. Y'from Italy or somethin?'

'Brooklyn'

'Y'don't say...Form is simple. Jus sign here...'

Simple? Sure. Insurance heads off with credit card,
addresses marry telephones...
Symptoms last, with measurements and morning
sickness.

'Powder room's through dere. Jus slip y'things
Dere's a gown behin de door'

Dr Paul is awaited with sober knees and goose-
green skin...
The couch facilitates disemboweling by holding
horse heels in the air. Guernica!
She chooses a chair...

Debbie Robsart, cute in College, consents to sit for
the wall.
His children credentials, freckle faced, and soured
by lemon sorbet socks and fizzy frills...
Dr Paul does it by the book.

There are books besides, regimental, piped with
gilt, ordered not consulted.
Two dead flies at the window, unobserved by the
cleaner, are his burden of misfortune.

He enters, stomaching a clip-pad, with thoughtful
clicking tongue...
Fingers straggle pensive to the safe lapel, and
spatula...
The tapping toe peruses...ten seconds is chewing
gum, stretched ever longer...

'Date of last bleed was when did y'say?'

(The Ides of May I?)
'Fifteenth, last month'

He spins the Winthrop calculator (roulette reminder not to be on the links when stakes are drawn)

The belly-bolting, tumbling-tide-of- help-me-Father *could* be arranged to suit the Caribbean cruise...

The raft of verbal boundary nailed. The sails will circum-navigate with careless quipping ease...

'People do this everyday. Relax'

The concierge in clogs and crackling skirt, hoists limbs astride the stirrups, covers the calyx that hangs its shadowed head.
The un-tossed rose dies in the dark, and withers to the compass steel.

'You've got a pelvis for an Atlas'

He withdraws the gander beak and drops it in the cackling dish.

'That's it Marcel. Let the girl go free...'

The carcass thighs are soft; the vanquished body
drags itself over the sand to a hook.

Sunday- Key West.

I shall go hang on the Continent's tail, beyond the
Barfly at Sloppy Joe's
Heedless of his beard and belching, my oaths will be toes
in the aimless water...Nostrils to the brindled air.
Space will shimmer scents from Tenochtitlan.
Gold bracelets bind me to the suicide of Cortez.
I am lost, but I shall find. They will never follow me.

I shall tread juice from tobacco clippings, and watch the
old men spit.
Havana ola, in the speckled shadows of the straw
market, my feet in the ashes, my cheeks smeared with
clay, wanton, outcast like them.
I shall not lick or roll. I shall not have to work
I shall simply be there.
For a day.

I shall eat smoked mackerel, pungent with wood,
steamed by the water, in a tipping boat.
The heaving horizon I shall tame to undulation.
I have spoken. I shall swim.
I shall tip boat-barrel and glide among the hawsers of
forgotten hulks, black amid keels, menacing with
mouths. Treasure is forgetfulness.
I shall sink.

I shall surface like the mermaid seal, untouchable.
Drag my gleaming limb.
Lollop and skid on the board-walk to watch the taffeta
water summon the world to drink.
I shall squint through rust and bitumen.
Bite through my lip.

The surgeon sun will fit me legs, brace my back and
bandage my eyes.
I will be led to convalesce.
The gold gulf wind will draw me unobserved
past shutters, rocking chairs and limes.
The machismo of yesterday is a hat by the water's edge.

'Mein Gott, the tenant is bedraggled, das liebes Kind is fried...
She'll look like the lobster tomorrow...butter is for burns, but am I interfering?
I'll just leave the iced tea.
I hope she'll talk or something. What is it now that's changed? Something worse? Or better?
Inside somewhere I'm sniffing steel.'

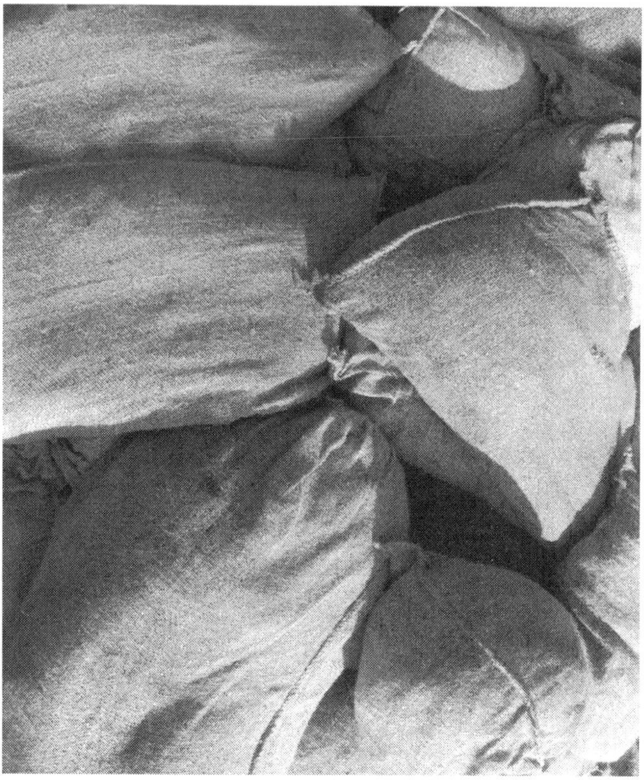

Monday- Brooklyn.

Guiseppe de Steffano is weighing cornmeal with
expansive fat fingers...
sniffing dust rising from the stoop, scoop-rolled
sacking of harvest.

For each creaking knee, a pound of bounty,
measureless calf nose, wet-stone, clinking
bucket-and-chaff intoxication...

There is a granary near Lucca...
but olive oil still to be pumped, safe for the
afternoon.

Women who enter are guests at the patron's apron
of white.
The groom of autumn leads on to the half ounce
paprika, two green peppers, half-a-pound tea.

'They have the appointaments, sure...
They have the new bambino, and will they feed it
properly? Encora...'

If they ask for salami, he wraps the weight of bells
in Bologna.
Pasta he sells with regret. It is so much better fresh

If they take also Parmesano, he will show the
machine that makes it easier...

'For the sake of the children, and the health of this God
forsaken nation!'

Of course the kitchens have no light, the windows
no cockerel burnished with sunrise,
the walls no vines, the eaves no dipping
swallows...
There is no gushing pump

'But Sancta Maria, an apron they can make!'

He has time for a view of the valley, and to stand for the Angelus.
Once a master baker, he now calls himself an alchemist.

'Cara, I sell art, not food...
Delicatessen! Never let me hear that word!'

He follows a dismal ragatsa, tugging her sulky son...courteous to poverty, and its second hesitation.
Gives *her* the apple, and slowly shuts the door.

He switches off the lights, stands and drops his head...
The gloom of day could be his farm stone store, but mice are there the movement that here is trickling rice.

Extinguished hospitality turns to blunt dispatch.

He cleaves six strokes of procuitto, wraps it in greaseproof, hangs a clean coat behind the door, latches and leaves for lunch.

....

Cara defers exactly at noon.

She ceases sorting index cards, slips an invitation
in the entrails of a book...
Removes some of her lipstick, but refreshes her
scent, ties a token apron...on afterthought knots
her hair; unbuckles wedge-heeled sandals, slips
into something flat...
Smoothes her generous bosom, moves unthinking
to her hip, catches herself in the unperturbed glass,
shrugs with sly chagrin...

Guilio will be tired. There's no need for anything

The provider lets himself in backwards, gracious to the Signora in the passage without. Acknowledgement is a habit he cannot learn to lose.

Cara clicks, slides waxed linen across the polished board; lays plates and large pressed napkins, knives and silver forks, pinches a radish from the salad, goes to bring in cheese...

Guilio appraises, shrewdly unconcerned, tonguing his teeth with his back to the view...

'Y'been out?'

'Guilio, of course not!'

'When do you go?'

'Perhaps later...I don't know...Come eat the lasagne, and after we have veal...'

He spreads his billboard napkin, tucks it in his tie. She kisses him roundly, and pinches both his cheeks.

They eat in virtual silence.
Most things are understood.

....

Cara leans thoughtless at the window, with hip and ankle flexed, drinking percolated coffee, with an idle cigarette...
Watching the insipid sun assault the robust haze to reach the middle chimneys, and at her feet, the street.

Her master has carried his plates to the sink, left his napkin on the chair rail...
Gone for an hour's sleep.

The day, left to itself, drags on a butt of air, snouts papers up contemptuously... kicks a tin can.

The garbage awaits the three black men.

Bell blast imperious!

The flaming roaring telephone drags Cara from miasma to strangle it in wool...

'Who is it?'

'Mama it's me. Oh Mama it's terrible...can you hear? Stephanie. Mama I'm pregnant...Mama don't talk... Wait let me tell you...Is Papa asleep?'

'Pregnant Madre Sacra, what the fuck does that mean? Pregnant, Sanctissima, so we all go to hell!'

The butter-solid silence, the metronome clock
times the breathing of Goliath on his gorse gold
bed...
The satin quilt slithers, subsides upon the floor...
Do springs betray intention?
He is still asleep.

Cara winds the long reproach of her daughter's
quiet life in a solid skein of anger, a loop of perfect
purpose, a rope, an unsheathed knife.

'It simply is not possible, and I do not want to hear...'

'Mama who are you? Can I...'

*'Listen I have said. It simply has not happened and he
must never know...'*

Compressed control hisses, the diamond backed
hand becomes a fist of certainty.
There is sting in the twisting ring.

'Mama I cannot'

*'Oh yes you can, for the sake of your father. He's a
wonderful man...
Also for Enrico who thank God is in Genoa...'*

'Enrico mama! That is all absurd...'

'It is your father's dearest hope... Since you gave up on College you owe him that, at least. We must return to Lucca... Now you must do it soon...'

'It is only legal in New York'

'What you are going to do, no-one can legalize...but you must not come here.
Ring me when it's over. Then you go away...
I have many things to think about but first
I go to pray...'

In silence sycophantic the apron is untied...
Swift scrolls of supplication wrought in iron bars of lace.
She hangs two rings with the duplicate keys, and carefully lets herself out...
She will not wait for the elevator, no, she will use the stairs.

The Park

Am I imprisoned in this kiosk of crude history?
The crossroads of ancestral hope confounded by a pin of chance?
Shall I carve my grief's graffiti?
While my stomach sings like grasses by the sea, bewildered?

Am I dumb and senseless captive creature
that I doodle with the pencil point of pain,
while the spaces roundabout
monument this mockery?

The metallic landscape is impervious
to bubbles frothing anonymity...
There is always more of pain.
The grasses will go singing to infinity...

It is now six, almost.

At six there will be people in the park...
Not the drip-dry shirtwaist and neckerchief duos on the benches leaping to arrest the wheel of imminent concussion.
Those will have packed the juice bottles and gone home.

Up in the dog-eared shade the swings will whisper-tip in melancholy echo of the afternoon's brief impulse...

The static giraffe may yet crane its neck to
challenge the energies of rowdy boys, but those are
not the ones she needs.

Nor else the Senior Citizens in banded hats, who
pace the last long fingered ball, and bend to
speculate upon a lie of grass, that elongates the
image pleasantly...

*'Maudie y'know has real slim wrists...If only she'd make
the effort...*
*Arthritis ain't the end of the world...Why, plenty of
folks go about with sticks.'*

No. Below the belt of sloping trees, the ground is
flat to take the rummage of impromptu ball.
The Hey-Here-Wow! of young blood blurring the
boats, stripped to shorts and drum beat skin...
watched by bare-back girls, with swinging breasts
under scarves of poinsettia silk.

Clay pressed collar bone, coil of ear, a kiss of sleek
sun-sculptured hair...
Mirage-maidens collectively, the distant voices
modulate...
Approached, it splinters into purses, apples, fags
quick darting glanced appraisal, then nonchalance
contrived...

They mostly know the name of the game.
Some play for real. Some observe and grin.

....

Sim and Josh are brothers, unalike, yet drawn by their acknowledged differences, to share with tacit time-content, a garage wholly welcoming.

Music is its core, mattresses its skin,
there are good girlie posters and a broken john.
Their clothes need patching, sneakers are worn
through, but there's coffee, wine and more often
than not, Hungarian food.
Sim is no mean cook, on the primus he nicked
from a chemistry lab

*'Nadia, god bless her, was my inspiration. Legs like
Marlene, and breasts t'make ya sing.'*

Josh is always silent, the water to Sim's thirst, to
his cornstalk, glade.
He gently plucks ' Petroushka' on the ribs of his
concave chest, takes another swig of coffee and
stretches his long legs.
His body is deficient from long pursued neglect.
Sim has calories enough to feed his lassitude.

They weight each other's balance, avoid each
other's girls.
Together idly speculate upon the squawk of
birds...

*'All that flesh yonder, and the splendid motion of those
things!'*

'Wrap it up Sim. I have no appetite'

'Did ya bring the frisbee?'

'Sure thing'

'C'mon then...if they join we'll see them swing...
Halleluiah honey...Ok, Ok don't sweat...
It was just a way of saying y'look good enough to eat.'

Stephanie skirts the nail-buff, match-flick, lie-
down, roll over fledglings.
In no mood to reflect or disclose

She hedge hops for the shade, where Lisa and her
little son hold guttering candles out for Sim...

Way over yonder he removes his shirt, stretches
and then throws a flawless curvature.

The frail and freckled mother squints against the
glare, adjusts her slipping headband, knocks the
tower...all fall down.

'Hey, how are you?'

'Why hi Steph...we don't often see y'here...Come sit
down a second...No, Philip, you've had one'

The two year old diversion makes it easy to begin,
to crouch, to squat, to find yourself sitting with a
spade.

'He's really growin bigger'

'Yeah, he eats an awful lot...No, Philip, mama
said...What the hell honey, sure, you go ahead'

The tilting toddler sets off towards the man, trips over an exposed root, gets up and carries on.

'Lisa, tell me really...Is it easy...y'know...on your own?'

'What? With a kid? Sure it gits like second nature... Why? What made y'ask?'

'I'm expecting.'

'No! Y'poor thing...Don't honey...
Don't consider it...For God's sake git it fixed...It'll finish all y'chances...might as well resign...
I know Philip's gorgeous...but if I hadn't had him, I'd have done it differently.'

Philip's clamour in the distance is more visual than heard.
Sim hoists him on his shoulder, ignoring the wet pants, hey up, comes giddy-up galloping over the grass...

'There y'are...go to Mama...she needs ya...hell she don't...

'Sim meet Stephanie, Stephanie, Sim...Let's hear it from the horse's mouth, Tarot-tell time...advice for a girl in the family way?

'Hitched to a steady fella?'

'No'

'Then I don't really see a choice...Ten minutes and sixty dollars is really all it takes...So, y'ave no money? What kinda excuse it that?
You only have to say the word...Josh and me'll pass the hat...'

'Thank you'

'Don't thank me. Belongs t'all of us...S'long Lisa...meet on Thursday Steph?
Now you be good, young man...Ok Josh, wowee, watch it, here she comes...'

With a Truckee - Hitching North

'Bye bye Miss American Pie
Drove ma Chevy to the levee, but the levee was dry...
An good ole boys were drinkin whisky an rye
Singin this'll be the day that I die... This'll be....'

'Gum?'

'Thanks.'

'D'ya sing?'

'Why d'ya ask?'

'Dunno. Helps some.'

Everglades awash with saw-grass to the borders of peachy Georgia; the smoke grey road cuts the water-flow.
It was laid by the card-sharper's hand.

'Who would've thought there was money in it?'

'There are always them as do.'

'You would've had to wan'it bad.'

Yonder St Augustine. Over the scales of the alligators into the arms of the ladies with lace fans and satin caps...

'Whoops...easy now... and the silver salver for the
collection, our heritage an all...
Pay no mind to the Seminoles...we pay 'em fur the
wrestlin...an most of 'em are tame.'

There are bird hides out on the flats, for them as
can stand the mosquitoes, the ever murmuring
midges...
To spy through the heat the spearing fish fowl,
drying its wheel-spoke wings.

The spoonbill imitates the sloth.

The heron simply blinks.

Buzzards are doggone dust in the eye, mayhap
you'll brown up a bear...

The heat is a white welt on the skin, and the silence
a sting in the ear.

'Whew...can you reach me some ice from the bucket?'

'Sure. What you gonna do?'

'I tie it around the back of m'neck...y'git cool...y'also git
wet...'

'Y'oughta get air conditioning'

'Try tellin 'em that in Vermont.'

T for Talahassee. If its neither chrome nor concrete,
it's hibiscus or a swinging seat.
Evenings are blister crackers, cambric, cottage
cheese.

'D'ya ever stop?'

*'Sure...bouta mile. I'll buy ya a sundae...D'ya like coffee
ice-cream?'*

'Prefer pistachio...coffee's ok'

*'Pistachio looks like peppermint...it's a cheat...but
y'have what y'want'*

Into blue-ridge County, heat haze moonshine, and
the mythical hillbilly boys, all bib-tucker freckle,
gawn t'ground in Nashville Tennessee...
only the sparse spine mountains, followin like
pickpockets, kickin each others heels.

On the local station, nuthin but down-beat denim,
nasal as snot...

'Ah reckon Ah could do as well.'

'Could you take that kinda trouble?'

*'Nah. Helps thinkin y'could. Ah'm gonna pull off in a
while and git me forty winks'*

'I'll take a walk'

'Watch out fer rattlesnakes...'

'I ain't planning to get to Nevada'

'They ain't the kind I meant.'

Vaulting down from vantage height, she bites the two-bit dust.

'Shoulda warned ya'

'I'm ok'

'Sure y'are'

Into the scrub forest where the giant shadow falls...
to raise the bracken battalions with their desiccated bows.
They release the tent-peg silence with one rising ringing dove...
An abyss of cool acceptance, unquestioning as sleep, oblivion in peeling bark, shedding the fixed grin...
Wet root, wet back, burying your face in green

God is the groin and armpit of tree,
(A chrysalis revolves on a thread)
His belly is the sweating earth,
His breast a nettle leaf.
Oh Sepulchre! Stone silence

Maria, comfort me...

'C'mon let's git. Five hours should do it.'

Gethsemane

'Located conveniently in the suburbs' it said.
So it is, in this two-eyes-and-a-nose sniveling
street, each eye with its twitching lid

Special offer for you lady, you and your yap-yap
animated pipe cleaner, tarred about the nose and ass...

Is it only your red-eyed dawg that weeps? Do you knit
as we pass by?
Holy Mary...Mother of God... pray for me now and in
the hour...'

Death? C'mon? Who said anything about death?

Twenty two, buckle-my-shoe. That mini-brick
incinerator ready for count-down?

That ain't nuthin but a postal depot for unclaimed mail,
sorted and stacked.

Dachau they thought was a bone-meal plant.

So it was.

What do they do with the corpses? Sixteen an hour,
eight hours a day, six days a week?

Holy Mary, midwife, mother, do you hold a murdered
baby by its feet?

'Second floor at the top of the stairs'

Calvary at least would give you time to think, and if it
were a sharp-stone path you'd need to watch your feet...
God, do you care when we thirst? When we twist?
Doesn't. Never did. Fuckin doesn't exist.
Mary, bleedin Mary knows, but she just sits and
weeps...
When, oh when will someone somewhere speak?'

'That's right. In here...Now sit y'self down. We've all
been waiting for the eighth to form the group...'

Seven febrile spinsters sit and suck their cheeks,
extenuate, then elongate, in the bowl of a
quivering spoon...
Shouting into silence, sinking into sibilance, with
canny careful grins...
They are clad in colour

All colours here are black.
All movement is mechanical.
All gestures calculate.

'Come in, sit down, we are expecting thee...'
The high priest dons his black mass mask,
prepares the surgery...

'Say, y'know...I find it kinda close...I'll jus open the
window so we can breathe a bit...'

The embroidered air hums an octave of sea.

the notes are single salted, threaten to dissolve...
benedictus, benedicat, the embedded memory!

Two feet on a beach with phosphorescent skin,
immaculate with winking rings on nail, on
anklebone...
The exploding dawn, the hissing surf, the welling
wet mud...
Further off the tip-toe crab that drinks the timely
surf, washed back from apprehension, and the
terrors of the earth, to float beneath a carapace,
and withdraw its periscope.

The blue bottle water, and all that lovely lace,
squandered on the menstrual moon, with her
hidden and pouting face.

If torn, it re-forms.
If tattered, it refracts.
When the scurrilous sea abandons it, it furs the
collars of the earth...

***'Meaning is in Being. Unconscious that you Are.
Willing is distortion.
I am neither near, nor far...'***

*'Oh God! Thank God! I could dance or weep.
Oh Lord forgive my anger, blessed Jesu, bear with me.'*

*'Now honey, never mind. Have a Kleenex...don't you
cry. You'll be through in half-an-hour...it really doesn't
hurt....Now where's you goin?'*

'Is this the way out?'

'You looking for the powder room? Honey, are you sick?

'No I feel marvellous. I just want the street'

'You wanna leave? But what about your fee? You came all the way from Florida...'

'It was worth it. I promise. You go on without me.'

Going Home

Hawk. High strider.
For whom do you churn buttermilk, who drinks your cloudless cream?
What power tilts your balance of wing?
Would you give no thanks for my shoulder of rest?

I'd give my right hand for your eye, for your nest,
for your claw of calamity, a beak-full of blood,

to spring without falter, to dip without guilt...
Hawk, sky serpent, will you teach me intent?

Salmon salut. What penetrates your impervious skin,
your scales of incision, your pivoting fin?
Fish, can you listen while you swallow the tide
convert the sea's order, placate its demon?

Stay steady and answer, while you sieve through a gill
as fine as a feather, the Omnipotent Will.
What gave you the courage to defy, single handed, the
Flood and Creation?
Salmon leap up and teach me to swim.

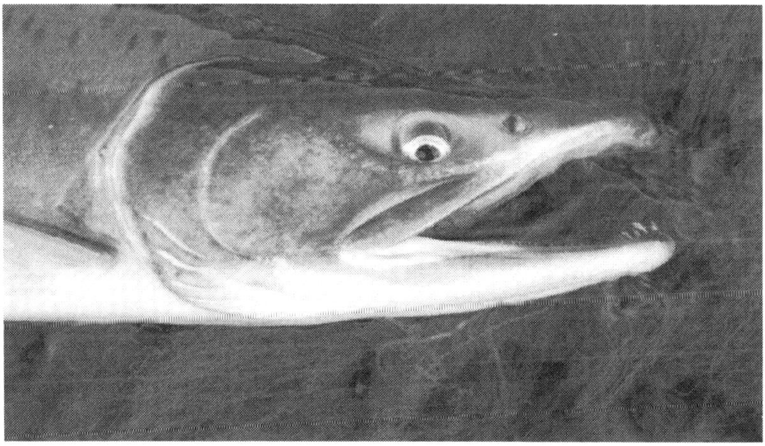

Fawn, frost-bitten, born before spring;
unprepared for extinction, without scale or wing.
From the muzzle of your mother, you steam your rough
faith that springs a quick skip to the grass's bent
swath...
Show me the marrow of innocence.

In the vortex of the waters we shall need the salmon's
skill;
in pounding confusion, the hawk's high pennant quill...

Child, when you set me from your shoulder,
Will you teach me how to live?

The Landlady

Miriam Martins is eating bagels off the blue
checkered cloth that gives a laundered look to the
wilting morning.
It is ten only; already the trees flag and hang out
their tongues...

I should sit all day with a fly whisk under a banana leaf,
is it so hot!
Like a native of the South Seas, all beads and belly
comfortable, with the sweat running into a rag.
Why do we whites make such trouble for ourselves?

The day yawns its intention to sleep.

The gate-latch chirps like an irritated cricket

Who is this, abroad before the morning is decent,
before it has taken out the curl-papers and pared its
nails?
Is that the tenant, so help me?
The girl who left a letter of no meaning wrapped around
the rent?
And I believing she was dependable...
Footsore...you can't fool me, stepping careful of
blisters...

Arthritic fingers fill the kettle.
The unswerving eye escapes the sockets of
prejudice, and annotates with sympathy

The younger generation have we betrayed,
solitude too much, too soon. The answers we had, but
did we first ask the questions?

'And nu? To pull the sheet over your head I'm sure, but first coffee, and you eat a little something...'

'Mrs. Martins I'm sorry'

'Sorry you should be, but later. Come. Come inside and sit down...if that cat should be so kind...a stool for the feet...the dirt never mind...some things are easy...'

Stephanie sinks into new observance, unclouded by timidity, or the over-ready answer.
An old woman dwells in dreams, and pokes the coals of neglected opportunity, without guile or expectation.
Her heart too huge to handle, threatens to boil.
She covers it with chatter.

'The grocer now is selling up...with the extra penny every time, should I be surprised?
Oi veh, but the coffee was, for celebration, a quarter off...but still fresh, you will taste'

She strains, pours and slides it across, sets bagels on a plate, aslant with knife and napkin...

'So eat'

The interrogation lies folded in elbows and the minute pursuit of crumb. It can wait.
Solicitude must first be fed, and is replete with the wiping of the mouth.

'Better huh?'

'Much. Thank you.'

'For thanks you can tell me where you've been?'

'I went to New York'

'To see your mama? Why didn't you say?'

'I didn't go home.'

'That is serious, to New York and not home? Miriam you are no fool, for a week something wrong.
For what good reason is a person going quietly to New York?'

'I went for an abortion.'

Apprehension finds no nest in this hospice of candour, where slanting sun embraces womanhood

'Now she tells me! Afterwards she tells me! Alone, living in my house, she gets an abortion without telling me!'

'I didn't go through with it.'

'So, with my own ears I must have surprises! A pregnant woman sits and eats bagels and feels perhaps, a little sick. She drinks coffee with a refrigerator full of

milk...She says nothing...Still she says nothing. Blood from stones, would you believe. So what are we going to do?'

The morning has moved apace to deliver
premature. Reminiscence trembles in the afterbirth
of day, and prophecy foreshadows dark.
There is instantly all and endless time for the old
woman, the young, and the obliging idiot clock.

Speech must now grow from silence, and the
stones that cockle the black backs of women in
prehistory, left alone with the consequence of men.

There will always be light on the sea;
rocks to serve for washboards, and make wrecks.
Children to hide and seek through lives...
Women remain, to spin the flax of deep
unquestioning.

'What are we going to do' was never a question,
but the birth of a design...
To fashion a key pattern, blood must serve for dye.

Two women bask in silence,
absorb the anguish sun.
The cradle of compassion lies in an open palm.

The Wisdom of Solomon

My world is swaddled in bandages, wheeled in a crescent dark boat.
It splints its feet in knitted boots, its fingers shackled in lace.
Its candid eyes are pin-tucked skies...
but patchwork scars its face.

Oh for a lifting lung and the slip-stream escape from the wave!
I would be anything but human.
Have we wriggled so far to be snared in warm blood
featherless, to assume dominion over those that are free?

Free to succumb in unthinking endeavour
A nest too slap-happy for wind,
an unduly severe winter...
a dearth of flying food.

Foresight and intelligence!
Why not beak or claw?
The well polished horns of conflict
impale all skidding hope.

I can choose what has been chosen, confine a bright bold
life in a barred cell of circumstance, fed on a selfish
breast of fierce and dogged watchfulness.
A twisted spoon of anguish, to feed skimmed, or curdled
milk.

My love I will set you afloat in a basket of weed
Commit you in prayer to the eddying sea...

My life will be brined in well bruised salt
It will numb the fluent tongue.
The songs it sings will be fractured strings.
Its colour sponges of grey.

But the moon will slice six blades of blood
first, my darling one.

The Agency

Coral Gables denies its origins with emphatic
upraised palms.
Too many flags oblige in its ascent, pay homage to
its marshalled loyalty...
(The State of the Nation here is manifest.)

The ancestry of mangrove mud is overlaid with
lawn.
The dugong, menaced by machine, is long
deceased.
No gentle jaws plough the navigable channels
free...

Where ocean-going fishing boats now snub the
wharf, the sinewed swarthy boy once clothed his
hook...laid his baskets, set his snares, and slept.

Here impeccable shutters are the well turned cuffs
on sleeves of houses, suites of rooms, textures in
two pleasing tones...
Wide sweeps of water, incised by steps, lead the
harnessed eye.

No hedges interrupt, or hold the small vulgarities
of yours or ours...too trimmed, or not enough...

'This neighbourhood b'longs t'all of us. Elected
residents and income keep the nigras out'

Women here have too much time to spend
entirely.
Despite the rigours of perpetual war with heat,
the car seat covers, and the sweat that lies in
ambush for the moment in unplanned transit
between the 'Charity Luncheon' and the 'Lonely
Wives.'
Good works and social conscience frost the day
that otherwise would be all angel cake

....

Adoption volunteers are all discreet, as befits the
empathy of those who ligature the cord, from
which the nerves run silver into smiles, and
thanks, and letters of content.

(The wound the new child left remains unstitched.
The bleeding staunched with words of cold
encouragement)

Before the blind and monitored transplant
the vessel must be nurtured carefully...
Tremulous questions answered with restraint...
the liquid of despair drawn to resolve in the
chalice of a healthy pregnancy.

....

*'A taxi we take. I pay, and I come too...You call and fix
it...I fix orange juice'*

Two women extricate from the comfort of the turning wheel...

Deliberate....

Conceal misgiving in elaborate concern.
(The Cuban cabbie rests his anchor arm athwart the brown split back)
They recount coins, check purses, pull at sleeves...
(He tips his mirror, wipes his forehead, sets the meter, and sits back)
The old one gives a tip with emphasis.
(He smiles and touches his baseball cap. Restarts the engine, waits, and pulls away to join his colours to the odds-on race)
The older takes the younger's arm, and forces a slower pace.

....

One was expected.
Another chair is fetched, the tapping point of irritation laid aside.
The sleek combed head shakes free its wasp of doubt, and smiles upon the Negro coffee maid.

'This must be your...? How very nice...How pleased I am to meet you...'

'She's a friend'

'Might as well be father for the way I feel...If I am speaking out of turn you put me straight.'

'Her name is Mrs. Martins'

'Miriam will do, and sick at heart to watch this tragedy...lovely mother...lovely girl come here to pledge her unborn child away. I come to say the things she cannot say herself, no shame it is, and no embarrassment...For love she comes to talk. Too old I am, to offer anything...If I had youth, or money...Ah my Gott'

The old face crumples like a burning shoe, and
shakes as though to free itself of scald.
The girl kneels to take the thorny hand; restore its
life against her wet soft cheek...

Two figures captured in the sculptor's eye,
weighted with grave linen-fold to drop the bowed
old back on slim arched neck...
finds unexpected stillness that shouts back.

Weeping assumes a flawless cast, and every
running tear an edifice.
Three women find themselves conjoined, by
wholeness and the single heart
Nothing was evaded. Nothing planned. A well
was struck. Three women drank.

Nothing now cannot be said. Little need be, either.

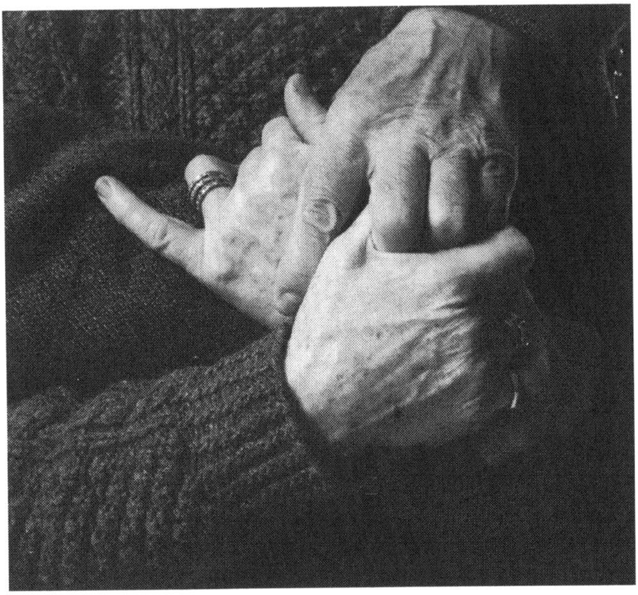

There is a house in the hills where expectant mothers wait, splitting and sharing the kindling of hope, and rocking their babies to life...

Curved bellies precede the slow paced day, and announce the imminent hour; paring, cooking, preserving fruit, searching the wide white sky.

Until they are delivered, their unmolested dream may seed itself in prayer, and fruit in lasting health...

'If I were you I'd go there, it's the only chance you'll get...to be alone together...If money is a problem we could subsidise...'

'That kind of money I can find. Now when can she go?'

'As soon as she can pack her bag'

'Without her mother, it's the best we can do...Take it darling...I shall be happy to think if I can do nothing else, I can, at least, do this. Promise Miriam one thing...You will try to be happy...hold your fat stomach and sing. Set the child up for happiness, somebody else can knit.'

The Dream of Childhood

In an orange orchard, Stephanie succumbed to a
scent, lethargic even for bees, and dreamt a dream
through the grasses of over-ripe summer.
A mirage trapped in honey.

Lying in a basket under olive trees, the lucid
perception dissolved the slight wind on her
tongue.
The sun through wicker, bristled her cheek.

The trees above were vivid with advice, their
supplications threaded on glaciers,
their consolations beads along branches...

A naked baby boy breasted the hay-stalks on solid
certain feet, handed her a wooden bowl, touched
her forehead and laughed...

Light plaited stalks into shadow, flickered its
tongues of warm snake.
Teased the clenched palm into opening...
She caught nothing but air, air to spread on her
face...on the tongue delirious, cool in the damp
warm neck.
Air was spinal ecstasy, air was bubble-blown,
vapid blue space.

Green was willow, willow, willow...
Light a prism of shifting cell.
Water the drifting necklace of leaves that swung
from the throat of shade

Water was water below, below the ankle-flex, sun-happy toe.
Light was water sound.
Music the coloured hexagonal beads, that pass between sky and ground.

The outstretched finger of cypress reached for the
thimble sky.
Dim with fledgling purpose, then began the
inchoate sound...
All sound, nacreous sound...
Over sand the sibilant sea,
the low moan of bark before curling,
the crack of whip branch rending, the booming
forest at eve.

Where sound and sight parted, there ploughs the
milk white ox, steady as leather, foggy as stone.
Harassed by the axle, tailing the shivering joist,
wading through the barking dog, tossing the
restive fly.

Nights are cloth soup silence.
The pressure-lamp hiss like a wasp churning oil
trapping space, asthmatic for air.
Un-consoled by the hammer tap-tapping of shoes
which when stilled, blow a ring of bright face.
Causing the dancing arms to blur, and shadows to
leap and curse.

Space is a sharpened pencil that writes a regular
day: White linen snapping at the grass, water at
heel to the pump.
The sky subservient to the brim of a bonnet,
the mouth to the resolute spoon...
Only the wind remains urchin, flying music, and
booting the moon.

Stephanie woke to a smouldering afternoon,
pregnant with thunder.

The Storm

A woman, now conscious of weight
she stands on articulate feet
to meet the curling whip slip wind, with a hitched
up petticoat...

Pinned and poised on a vertical thread
a dryad is drawn from the earth
to spindle the light from the anxious trees, she
begins to slowly rotate.

Flashing quick iridescence, she holds the prism of
fear.
Eddied from greenwood, tossed, caught, thrown
forward from branch to branch like a firework
trailing smoke.

It dies with sudden indolence snuffing its candle
tongue, awaits an insolent frisking, by the heedless
back-slapping wind...

It comes.
She takes it standing, welcomes its hands up her
skirt.

Smells its moist breath searching,
shakes her hair in eloquent spray,
lifts besotted arms in worship, grinds her heels in
the mesmerized clay.

Appeased, it retreats smiling, licks resin from the
split in a stone.

She stands in the whirlpool of luminous light,
while trees discard bright fruit, to roll like luscious
jewels, and break open on the grass...

Trepidation, thirst, devotion bind these barren
bearing folk while...
the prodigal squall dallies in the distant thunder-
smoke.

Focussed on by frenzied clouds wielding a
blinding knife...
harassed by quivers of showering steel from
archers massed on the flank...

Fatigued by peccadilloes with young larches,
nubile corn...
He gathers his full manhood to shake the
shoulders of the earth...

The landscape lies down.
Spreads its limbs, and turns its head.
The cumulus mainsail darkens, lifts its scudding
skirt, boils the seas in anger, braces a hidden keel...

Imploring hysterical insects fret at a cello string...

His teeth sink in earth's jugular.
He swiftly snaps her back. Crack.
Wraps his thighs about her, and drenches with his seed.

Drowning she drinks from a bottomless thirst while he loves her from his elbow, and cracks his silver whip..

Bone snap, neck lash, back, back, back.

Hounds chained to his chariot, growl on blood-lust bent; his eunuch plumed horsemen are shod with kettledrums.

The immaculate artillery sprays the gusted arrows, pause, refit, and swing up-wind... following with dentist drills, the skittish novice breeze...

Slaps her cheek
Stings her eye
Beats her buttock
Bites her thigh
Then fulsome and unstinting takes her open mouth...

....

In love's apotheosis, the battalions withdraw,
evaporating into cloud, with grumbling after-
thought.
Cracking one slow rolling rump, spitting, not quite
spent...
leaving rain to cherish bruises, bitten in torment...

Soft, he lifts up every weeping leaf; licks each
saturated bud.
Bathes pain and past together in mercury and salt.
Rests his quivering nostril in her aromatic ear
Whispers unbelieving joy and strokes her rivulet
hair

Fragments of Fortune

1
Duck-dipping head, redoubling fist;
down the bottom of the river kissed.
Here must I sit eating berries from my hat
at the elbow of the river, while you nestle in its lap.

2
This wide boarded room, barred by reflected light,
imprisons time in whispers, between the clattering
of cups.

All of time is curved, concave or convex.

Future time floats forward, only held in check by
the muscle of this moment and the bow of bended
neck.

The past is expressed in the crook of candid knee
reminiscing over toenails, and the interrupting lap.

While the curve of time present falls across the
patient cheek;
the loop of threaded needle, the sprung
embroidery hoop.

In the aspic of the present that congeals time's
clear straw blood, is pulse and retraction, the
pump and suck of life.

Antecedent and descendent turn slower
somersault.
Each swallowing the other's tail, confined in
Now's torn heart.

But tell, from where you see it, upside down...
Are we standing on our heads?

3.
Your life has been gathered in this scented orange grove,
(bridal flower brought to fruit), and in pomander, clove.

Birth

At evening, out walking, gravity plucked at her back.
A pain like the stroke of a rowing eight was raised by her surprise...
Doubting, she continued under the gothic sky.

The barefoot forest dug its feet deep in layered leaves...sniffed guardedly at mosses, reticulate with green.
Cold water ran, still sluggish, over the lip of stone.

Bark clutched at wisps of lichen shawl.
Twigs picked frosty teeth.
Only the drifting fog at her feet was pungent as briar smoke.

Insensate spring drowned in dream under a skin of milk.
All of growing saved its breath to bite her clotted lip.

Only garrulous crows coming to rest clattered keys in the canopy.

From a lonely farm on a swirling hill a single dog barked, sharp.
The gruel of a day in winter congealed the larded moon.

In a cold chancel of leaded glass, the women with imminent child knelt down and pressed her face to the earth.
History accepted her.

A root took her slim wrist.

The midwives of the forest gave the sweet dark soil to sniff.

The seasons of the future roped her amphibious waist, drew the slip-line tighter, grazing the forks of trees, tethered the halter of coming calf in the throat of the unplumbed sea.

(The rope was a five ply nerve, clamped with strong white teeth. The intrepid monkey-muscle would follow it, through gasping and sweat and help-me-God into and out of death)

All this prepared in stillness, in the screed of the darkling wood...
Builders in the fan vault dropped two feathers at her feet.

....

Stephanie bit the threads of reluctance, and lay down in the blanket leaves; determined to take the first stage alone, with the help of the awestruck moon.

She spread-eagled to contact as much as she could of the wiser belly of earth; harked to be taught by silence how to make love with death.

A last late pigeon shuttered the day, finally for sleep.

A hoot-owl beckoned the stars.
The dark rolled the sun in its sleeve...
The host of heaven would navigate the perilous
pass to port.

From a great height she spotted it, white foam on
her saucer sea, smelt an intangible waft of salt,
but it only washed to her feet...
Retreating without menace, it promised to come
back.

Watching, the night dropped rosary beads
rhythmically in her lap, eased its kneeling slightly,
blew softly on her scalp...

She sank into weightlessness, wandered into time
where colour was all summer...
Only thought was motion, and all of will was
freed.

This time the wave's crest finger drew her on like a
ring, pushed her over its knuckle, and settled her
in flesh.
She was fastened, and she knew it, on the blade of
a paring knife.

She steadied the rising fish-flash fear, and took
slower deeper breath.

Surgeon trees consulted, sprinkling water on her face.
The wind took her pulse with a turning leaf.
A night-jar threaded a song, single pearls of sweetness from the pod of splitting throat.

She held the hand of a loving log, who gently
braced her back.

The tide was coming in.
The swell now held a throb, the harbinger
of distant waves gathering out on the reef.

Defined by foam still singly, but successions now
in view...

She turned her mind to the prow of a boat, pitiful
small, probing the treacherous coral ring, seeking
its blind way through.

She would need to haul on the ropes of pain to
guide it into the lea; through a ring of bright fire,
onto the shuddering sand.

The forest acquiesced.
They had delved from the deep, a flawless
moleskin vessel, filled with God's right hand.
To vouchsafe it into Creation, they needed the
hand of man.

....

Flushed from the covert of the brush-beat wood,
Stephanie half ran...
Handed from pillar to nave pillar span, a pheasant
confused by a straight chalk line...
Time held panic on a running rein, flicker fused to
the tight-lipped sky...

until she crashed through bracken onto the moon-
washed lawn...

A scalpel nicked at her pelvis, and dropped a
cloudburst at her feet.
She waded through surf of her making, up the
steps of a porch...

Poseidon had escorted her over his figured prow.
Timely oarsmen synchronized his escape from the
sycophant shore.

She was abandoned to the little men in a soiled
and soaking skirt

....

The interior was linen paint, the floor a well-swept
bed.
She was pushed to a couch and climbed on it, like
a cat with broken legs.

This wave broke in a paroxysm...

All about were squeaking screens, and running
feet, and tubing, a syringe in front of spectacles...a
sudden jab in the thigh...

The merciless voices receded with the return of the
dignified sky.

Her head was inaccessible to confusion, panic, or shame...
She would bestow her body to kernel the child, and split from stem to stern.
Her tireless knees rowed boulders of pain which crushed her bones like rock salt, gnawed loose the links of her spine...

The cry of life escaped her, as in fire she crowned her king.

Then frog bright limbs swum from her, and she was floating in light....

'How is he? Oh how is he?'

'A perfect baby boy'

'Let me see, let me hold him...'

'No, my dear. That wouldn't be wise, or right.
Lie back, you've done a wonderful job...
We'll take care of the child.'

The feet that marched him under a sheet drained away all sense.
She simply stared bewildered when they showed her the afterbirth.

(They stitched, washed and brushed, and wheeled her to lie in the dark; brought her tea routinely, and gave something to help her sleep.)

While the galaxy broadcast new stars, Christopher slept in a plastic tray, under a pale blue shawl.

PART TWO

Post-mortem

In the clean swept chapel where the requiem was
wrung, baptism in light has left a watermark on a
transparent chalice with its liquid listlessness.

Lilac veins draw the opalescent bone, the fragility
of wrist and jaw, the clean clarity of gaze.

All of this distilled in milk, unconsumed and
trickling steadily...

....

Outside the trees accept the vestments of
methodical summer, daily obstructing more of the
sky.
Casting shadows to merge with the shadows of
clouds, pre-occupied with purpose that has its
acorn centre in harvest's half closed eye.

Leaving she, who felt she'd seeded it, beached
with grey salt rind.
A shell not yet stripped of its ganglion, moist in its
mantle, transparent as glass.

Trodden, half buried, by the passage of meals,
the changing jugs of water, the slanting leading
question, the surreptitious look.

Stephanie burns to extinction, un-protesting as
wax.

Discarded by the synchrony of her and nature's
pulse, she answers questions timidly, signs papers
without reading...
accepts the lunatic lie.

Starting like a dreaming dog when a hastening
tread at the end of endless corridor frees
a hiccoughing cry...

Tomorrow they take the baby away.
(She has gained consent to send an unsigned letter,
and a home made teddy bear)

When she has signed the last release, she'll be free
to leave...

Reincarnation

Miriam knits with wire fingers intermittently oiled
by nuts.
Persistence is a change of stitch, reward a needle of
salt...

*Oi veh! A bikini I might have managed, so for why do I
start a cape?
Midsummer now, it almost seems, and who knows if she
likes the shape?
A boy we always knew it would be, and a beautiful child
she said...that woman from the agency...but why can't
Stephanie write?'*

Distraction fills the kettle. The mailman is overdue.

*A letter it is, at long last...too short for any news...Mein
Gott she says she would rather walk!...but ah, in a taxi
she comes...This afternoon? Is it the ninth? And the
florist too far down-town...if only a nursery with nice
white crib...Now don't you start again...*

....

The black bull-terrier motor scents the rolling
redolent street...
Slows to claim an azalea outside number forty
eight...

A moment's frozen action drains the pneumatic pulse. Welcome becomes fearful, too elusive to define, the austerity of grief too wooden to succumb...
The familiar, now untouchable, purged in a foreign fire...

Unreachable, discalced, worshipful and meet, enclosed in skins of suffering, in themselves too sweet to be discarded easily...

The impulse that would rush to greet, and in exuberance obscure, is held to the doorknob by a thread of respect.

Nothing now can be assumed...

Except that all is new, built only on shared knowledge, archaic, inescapable, and bitter as the single time-scarred Yew.

....

'Ai, to see you, just to look at you is, for me, enough'

The spittle syllables fall like flares over artic wastes....

Stephanie drops her shoulder-bag.
Considers the sun on the parched back lawn,
the limb black mango leaves,
the stain of shade on the old settee...

Then she grasps the anxious waiting wrist, as if to nail with words. To spear hope or expectation with a hooked complicity

'You must realise I am dead inside, and I want to stay that way...
I shall destroy your generosity, because I cannot, now, respond...'

'So for what return have I ever asked? It is enough to care for you, of course you are alone. The food and comfort I prepare for you, must comfort me'

The puckered old mouth twitches, the apron's quickly smoothed...
Restraints, sharp reined, un-sluice the weir dammed by sympathy...

The gorged stomach of injustice heaves, all barriers collapse...
The old nurse finds herself close held to the mother's aching breast.

Infancy

Past weeks have been timeless with sleep, sedated
in dreamlessness; existence weighted beneath a
stone, cast in a still mill-pool.
The skin on the surface pricked by a nymph,
surfacing only to share the solace of meals, before
submerging again.

The future is shorn of impetus, the past of
relevance.
The quicksand of the present is a drugged
oblivion.

Miriam rocks, with tapping feet, pushing the
needle home
It is a ravelling of faith, that the garment will be
worn.

....

There are signs of dim intelligence, (the observance
of the squirrel's track down from the wire to the
wall); the foot outstretched to the threadbare
warmth; the start to the blue jay's call.

Nothing of news is newsworthy, no import far
from home...
The unthinking gaze is focussed on the edge of a
wrapping shawl.

So what do I do to resurrect where help is hopelessness?
The future must teach forgetfulness, but should she try to forget?
Life must go on, if it happens that way, there's no sense in aimlessness.
This afternoon we go for a walk, down to the beach and back.
If she resists I'll tell her straight...I need the exercise.

There is no hook to recover resolve from the bottomless pit of despair.
Lethargy, that toothless crone, skims perpetual indifference from the cream of richer care.

Convalescence must be shamed into shouldering its load.
Without the swinging carrot, it's like flailing at the dead.

Nevertheless it must be done.
Without slackening the rein, the stubborn white-eyed yearling, led to walk again.

Miriam, as smithy, blows on tempered common-sense.
Stephanie, wordless, accepts the fetlock's added strength.

'In two weeks, you go back to work...the routine will be therapy, unthinking, automatic...
In time you can think again...You've just had a vacation...Anyway, nobody will ask.'

Adolescence

Two days have been walked with a sandal step,
lighter for inconsequence and the competent salad
of hands.

Busy enough to free the mind to turn turtle in the wind.

The wind was unexpected, gusty and fresh off the sea, following her puppy skirt, sneezing, with overlarge feet.

The crossbred runt of a pedigree, remote in the frame of time, fickle precocious companion, joyfully reprieved from grief, to snout papers up the street.

It may come alright in the end.

....

Solitude is the centre of sane, in a circle of meaninglessness.
Activity transcribes an arc, that returns to itself when spent.

Alone I can move without shifting
Alone I can see and stay blind
Alone I can float paper boats down the tramways of cataract mind

Only talk, and the flick-knife question
The nailed boot, and sprayed shot of converse
leaves me insensate, raw, and pleading for a word to end all words.

I must learn to wait for the water. I must free my ear to vibrate.
I must accompany with moistened tongue, the voices of time and space.

But do not ask me to talk to the people, for I cannot discern what they say.

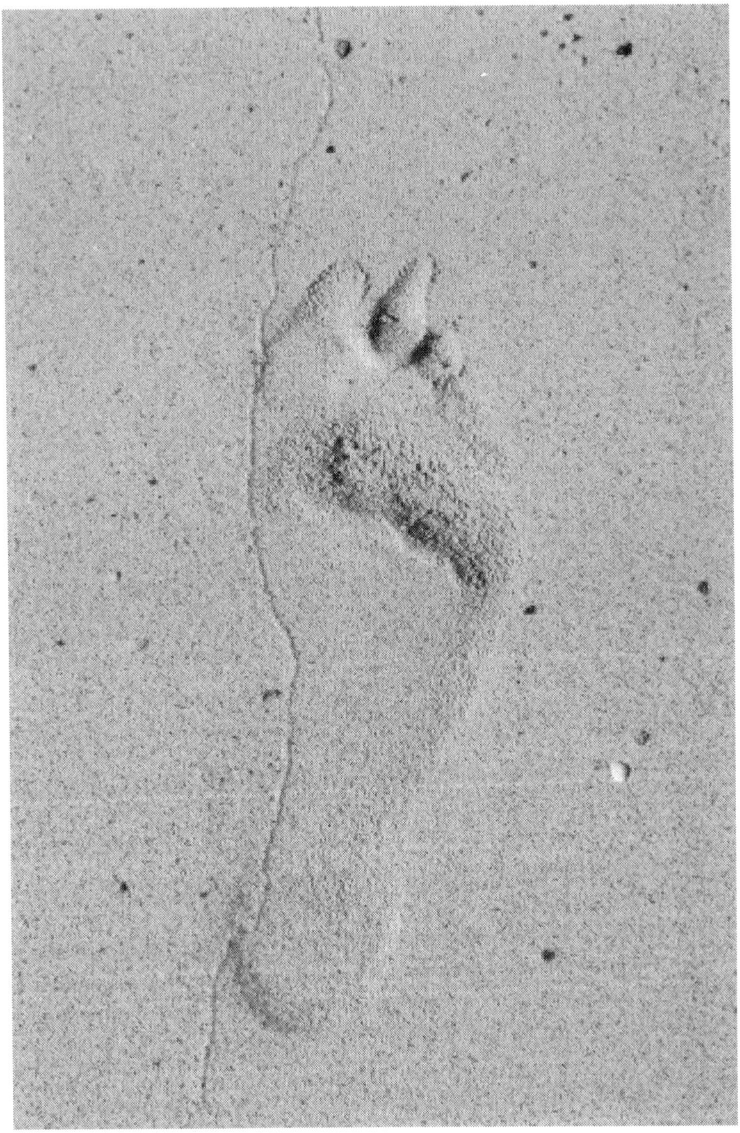

Maturity

On the third day, quick as a fox, came a woman in a brush of wind.
Soft-spoken and expensive, the scarf that fell to the floor was silk, and she recovered it, before she perched near the door.

She was directed soon to Stephanie, relieved by her air of haste.
She would not want trivial talk, and that was a relief.

Familiar from a distance, but more composed than before...
She looked...well neater...economical? It was hard to say...
Her crows-feet deepened when she smiled.
Younger, half-ironic?

No, more like half-amused.

Stephanie tied the gingham cape, and gently sat her back.

The hazel eyes in the mirror observed as she tidied the crown with the tail of a comb, before voicing a plea, with a click of deprecation and a part apology...

'I don't have too much time, I'm afraid, so could you just wet and trim it, and leave it to blow dry...It more or

less takes care of itself, and there's a good strong breeze outside.'

Stephanie followed the arc of the natural curl, by letting it fall from the comb.
Without further fuss rotated the chair, commenced to balance hot and cold, and deftly used the shower.

The pointed shears tapered the hair down to the nape and the cheek. Spicules of the glossy cap fell steadily and thick.

Fingers sifted a good loose scalp...

A palm pressed the neck into flex so the unswerving eyes in the mirror were extinguished in their sockets by the angle of the brow....

'It's sometime since you've had it cut, the ends are starting to split...'

'Yes I've been so caught up with the baby...I just haven't had a chance to venture out, to work upon myself.'

Stephanie slowed but continued, forcing herself to speak,

'They always say a baby plays havoc with your hair...still you wouldn't have it otherwise...and I guess having him compensates.'

The woman at these simple words suddenly seemed to expand, her thin shoulders that had sat four-square, melted into her lap.

'Oh he's a perfect angel, no real trouble at all...only he's asleep all day, and far too cheerful at night...Say would you like to see him? He's in his carriage outside. I try so hard not to be the proud mom...but I need the smallest excuse...'

'I don't think I should step outside. I haven't been back long...'

'Oh pay no heed to Renee, I've known her quite a while...Anyway I'll bring him in...don't worry now, you've finished...I reckon that'll do...'

Already she'd leant forward and was fiddling with bows.

Stephanie bent over to retrieve an irrelevant pin, straightened up decisively, and finished dusting the neck...
She untied the apron, swung the chair, taking two steps back...

'I'd love to see your baby'

'Good I'll go fetch him'

Still she hung like a marionette, suspended from a hook. No matter how she struggled she could not touch the ground...
while all around swum silent fish, on the other side of glass.

Mrs. Armstrong retreated, in a slim brown summer suit.
Her ankles were pared to articulate bones, her feet cherished in calf.
She bent for a word with Renee, who nodded, and then smiled... Laid her leather purse upon the desk, and disappeared outside.

The door swung to behind a crisply pleated skirt.

....

She returned a second later, with a sari of a shawl in the heart of which was a lily rose, leafed in finely spun lace...

In spite of confusion and panic, Stephanie gazed at the face, as smooth as a Flemish virgin, cool as the skin of a grape.
It had flushed on a winter of strawberries, and woken out of sleep...

It drew her like a truth in the night, and her feet into slow approach.

Renee bobbed and clattered

Idle girls all shuffled round

'Oh isn't he jus darling!'

'Ah really think he's cute'

'Say he has the littlest ears...'

Mrs. Armstrong turned to Stephanie

'Well tell us what you think?'

'I think he's very beautiful...' a small hand gripped her thumb, *'what name have you called him?'*

'Well his name is Christopher...but that wasn't up to us...that's what his mother had him called...we adopted him you see...
But you're my precious darling, aren't you my sweetie? She must have been a wonderful girl, you can see that he's been loved...she even wrote a letter... Wait, I have it in my purse...say, could you hold him a minute?'

She raised her cradle shoulder and dropped the child into his mother's waiting arms.

....

His glance was calm, uncurious.
He perused the new found face.
His pagoda gaze was a sage of sky, reflecting ancient pools, encompassing all, and un-perplexed.

He stilled bewilderment.

She, spiralling larks, and a hover of hawk, sank down upon a chair...

Christopher lay like a frond of green fern, across her lap of light, gripped her finger tighter, and paddled both his legs.

Nobody noticed the mother and child, communing and entranced.
Nor how reverently she stroked his cheek, and softly kissed his brow.

They were held in the palm of an upraised hand
in a circle of blessedness,
alone in a triptych of frescoed gilt...

While the letter was passed round.

Bandied for curious scrutiny, and a passage read aloud.

Stephanie flowed with infinite love which infused the golden child, who gently turned against her breast, and seemed to fall asleep, his long dark lashes feathering a curved and peerless cheek.

His breathing rose and filled her need...
She touched his blossom hand that had caught a minute finger through a hole in the spider's web.
His matchless peace invaded her.

She knew that they were one.

Mrs. Armstrong paid her bill, and suddenly looked round, disconcerted by the stillness of her son, asleep in the lap of a child.
Still as milk in the shadowed churn of the closing apricot day, the simple gingham overall evoked a nursery rhyme...

The goose-girl settled in feathers, by a barn, in the day's half light...
Her bare feet streaked with new cut grass,
her arms across sleek white backs...
Try as she might to suppress it, the image held her eye.

She clipped her purse decisively, threw words in mock alarm,

'Well it's no use falling asleep young man. It's time to take you home...'

Stephanie stood, and without lifting her eyes from his face, said

'There's no need to disturb him. I'll carry him outside.'

If you have enjoyed this book please consider leaving a review on Amazon or Goodreads. Your opinion matters.

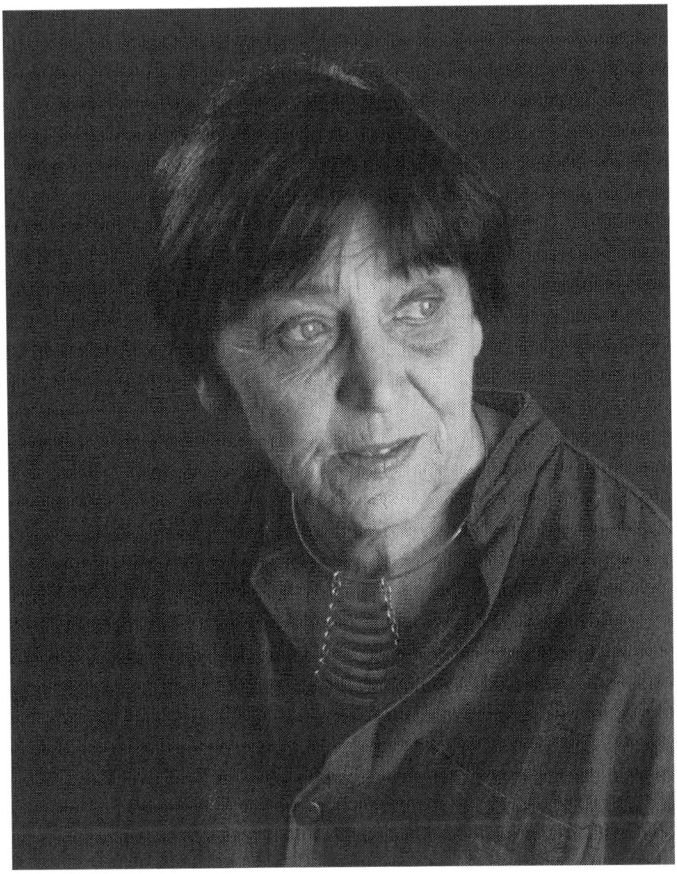

A Shadow in Yucatan (ISBN 978-0-9575002-3-5) may be ordered (signed) from Philippa's website http://involution-odyssey.com/
From Amazon UK **http://bit.ly/ShadYuc**
From Amazon US
And all ebook distributors (see website for links to relevant book pages)

'This was her first book to be published'

'Involution-An Odyssey Reconciling Science to God' was published by CollaborArt Books in 2013 and may be sampled on her website http://involution-odyssey.com/ where recordings and reviews are posted. It achieved highly commended runner-up nomination for the Book of the Year (2013) by the Scientific and Medical Network and has received notable endorsements from Ervin Laszlo, Philip Franses, David Lorimer and Andrew Harvey.

The website offers links to all retailers and books are available in both print and ebook formats.
http://involution-odyssey.com/ebooks-and-where-to-buy/

Philippa welcomes any contact or questions from readers and can be contacted at philipparees7@gmail.com